Violet's Big Bracelet

and the **Flowertots**

Created by Keith Chapman

First published in Great Britain by HarperCollins Children's Books in 2007

1 3 5 7 9 10 8 6 4 2
ISBN-13: 978-0-00-722595-8
ISBN: 0-00-722595-4

A CIP catalogue record for this title is available from the British Library.

Based on the television series *Fifi and the Flowertots* and the original script 'Violet's Big Bracelet' by Gillian Corderoy.
© Chapman Entertainment Limited 2007

Printed and bound in China

Violet's Big Bracelet

HarperCollins *Children's Books*

On the roof of Forget-Me-Not Cottage, Fifi was hanging out all of her washing but the line was looking very, very full.

With a loud PING, the line snapped in two and all of Fifi's wet clothes flew into the air.

"*Fiddly Flowerpetals,*" Fifi cried. She tried to tie the ends of the washing line into a knot but it was no good. "I'll just have to buy a new one."

"I'm sure there was something else I was supposed to do today," Fifi sighed, as she hopped into Mo and trundled across the garden.

Over at Honeysuckle House, Bumble was making breakfast for Fifi. Pip Gooseberry was scooting by when he saw the packed breakfast table.

"Morning Bumble," Pip said, wandering into Honeysuckle House. "Can I have some breakfast?"

"Not yet, Pip," Bumble said. "Fifi will be here soon. You can have some then."

But Fifi was not on
her way to Bumble's house. She was talking
to Violet, who was sad because she had run out
of beads and Poppy was on holiday

"Don't worry, Violet," Fifi said to her friend. "We'll think of something."

Fifi had completely forgotten about Bumble and her washing line!

A little gust of wind shook some seeds from the tall flowers above Fifi and Violet on to the floor.

"Flower seeds everywhere," Fifi muttered, then the idea hit her. "That's it, we'll use the seeds as beads! They come in all sorts of shapes and sizes and I know where we can find lots of them!"

"Oh," Violet was very excited. "And we can paint them all different colours!"

The pair hopped into Mo and drove off in a hurry.

"Look, Fifi," laughed Violet, "these seeds are square!"

"And these ones are a funny shape!" Fifi smiled.

Soon, Fifi and Violet were having great fun shaking the seeds out of dozens of flowers.

"This is so much more fun than just buying beads," smiled Violet. "Fifi, are you sure you've got time to help me?"

Fifi thought for a moment. "There was something I was going to do. I wonder what it was."

Bumble stood at his gate looking for Fifi. "I wonder where she could be," he muttered to himself.

Pip sat at the table, looking at all the delicious food. "We could start without her?" he suggested hopefully.

"Not until Fifi gets here!" Bumble said, patting Pip's hand away from the hot, yummy toast.

Fifi and Violet were very busy painting the beads they had collected. Primrose popped her head in the door of Flowertot Cottage. "What are you doing with these seeds?"

"We're going to make them into bracelets. Do you want to make one too?" Violet asked.

"I'm sure I was supposed to be doing something this morning," said Fifi, unloading the last of the seeds from Mo's truck.

"What could be more important than playing with us?" Primrose asked, moving on to the lilac paint. Fifi sighed. She knew there was something...

Bumble was really fed up. "Where can Fifi be?" he sighed.

"Never mind, Bumble," said Pip, eyeing the lovely food. "I'm here and I love breakfast. Fifi probably forgot."

Once they arrived at Forget-Me-Not Cottage, Bumble
soon realised Fifi was not at home. Outside, they saw all of
Fifi's washing hanging over the roof and inside there were
dirty dishes in the sink, plant pots all over the table
and a floor in need of a good sweep!

"Come on, Pip," smiled Bumble.
"Let's tidy up. It'll be
a surprise for Fifi!"

Fifi was still trying to remember what she was supposed to be doing that day as Primrose held up a beautiful bead bracelet.

"Who are these for, Violet?" Primrose asked.

"They're for your **best friends**" Violet explained.

"Then I'll definitely give one to Bumble." Fifi said. Suddenly she *jumped* up, spilling beads everywhere. **"Jumping Geraniums,** Bumble! He invited me to breakfast this morning and I forgot!"

"Well, why don't we go to his house now," Primrose suggested gently. "You can give him your bracelet to say you're sorry."

"Ok, Primrose," Fifi said doubtfully.

Soon, Fifi, Violet, Primrose and all their beads were at Honeysuckle House.

"Bumble!" called Fifi. "We've got you a present!"

But Bumble wasn't home. Fifi felt terrible. What if Bumble
didn't want to be her friend anymore?

Just then, Pip came skipping into the garden. "Fifi, there you
are!" he smiled. "Bumble made you breakfast but then you
didn't come so-"

"He doesn't want to be my friend
anymore, does he?" she sniffed sadly.

"So we took breakfast to your
house!" Pip said taking
Fifi's hand. "Let's go!"

"It's so tidy!" Fifi gasped as they arrived
at the cottage. "Did Bumble do this?"

"And I helped," nodded Pip proudly.
"Bumble's on the roof, mending the washing line."

"The washing line!" laughed Fifi.
"I forgot that too!"

Bumble was up on the roof, when Fifi came rushing at him.
"Oh, Bumble!" she began, "I was on my way to your house and
then the line broke and I went to the market and I –"

Bumble cut her off, laughing. "That's OK, Fifi.
I know you sometimes, ahem, forget?"

"You really are the best friend in the whole world!" said Fifi. "And we did make you a friendship bracelet."

But there was much too much for one bracelet!

"Perhaps we could cut a bit off..." suggested Violet. She quickly went to work with her scissors and made bracelets for everyone but there was still lots left over.

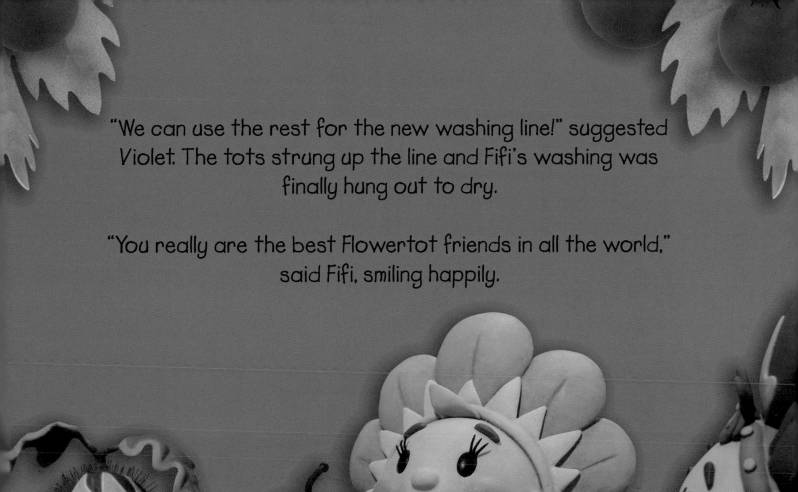

"We can use the rest for the new washing line!" suggested Violet. The tots strung up the line and Fifi's washing was finally hung out to dry.

"You really are the best Flowertot friends in all the world," said Fifi, smiling happily.

Make Your Own
Friendship Bracelets

Friendship bracelets are a lovely way of showing your friends how special they are to you. Makes lots and lots and give them to everyone you love.

You will need:
*Thick, coloured threads
*A round pencil
*Old newspaper
*Glue or Paste for papier-mache
*Paints

1. Cut a piece of coloured thread about 10cm long.

2. Tear the newspapers up into long, narrow strips then dab some paste down the length of the strip.

3. Wrap each strip tightly around the pencil into a small tube. You should still be able to slip it off, so not too tightly.

4. Once the bead is dry, slip it off the pencil and paint it in your favourite colours.

5. After the paint has dried, string the beads on your coloured thread and tie to make a bracelet. Now you can give them to all your friends!

You can use lots of different things for beads, pasta shapes, buttons, even seeds, just like Fifi!